D1632919
5430000511800 4

This book belongs to:

… …

Flora, Buxton & Bear

BEAR

and the

WOBBLY TOOTH

Rowena Blyth

Bear was cleaning his teeth. He took special care of them and brushed them **every** morning and **every** evening. But this morning, Bear discovered one of his teeth was wobbly.

He worried that if it fell out,
it would be gone forever,
and then how would he...

whistle?...

Or speak?...

Or eat?

In the park, he told his friends, Flora and Buxton.

“I really don’t want to lose my tooth – especially as it’s my favourite one!”

"Don't worry, Bear," said Flora, as she opened her mouth wide.
"My mummy says these are just our milk teeth.
They have to fall out to make room for our grown-up teeth,
which are even bigger and stronger."

"Really?"
Buxton and Bear
looked confused.

"Oh, most definitely, yes," declared Flora.

"When your tooth falls out, you put it under your pillow, and my daddy says that if you go straight to sleep – really, really quickly – the Tooth Fairy comes and leaves a coin for you!"

"And what happens to your tooth?" asked Buxton.

"Well," replied Flora, "the Tooth Fairy collects all the bright, shiny teeth and puts them in the sky to make it sparkle. My mummy says it's called the Milky Way."

"Ohhh," said Buxton and Bear,
as they stared up at the sky in amazement.

"And even better than that," said Flora excitedly,
"with the coin the Tooth Fairy leaves under your pillow,
you can buy anything you like in the
whole, wide **world!**"

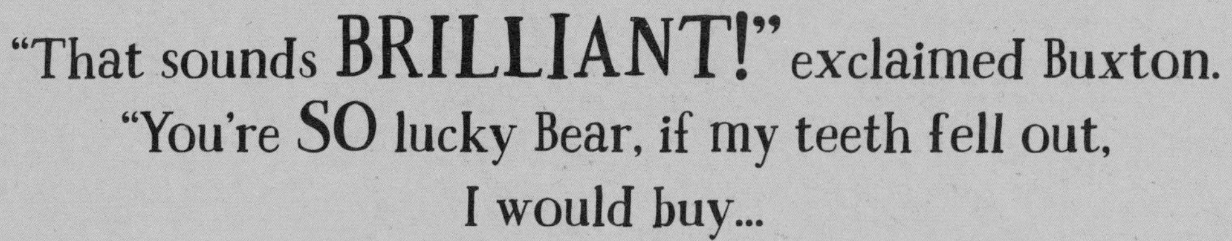

"That sounds **BRILLIANT!**" exclaimed Buxton.
"You're **SO** lucky Bear, if my teeth fell out,
I would buy...

ALL the cakes and cheese
in the supermarket!...

AND a dinosaur!...

AND a space rocket – so I can
fly to the Milky Way!"

"What are you going to buy with your coin, Bear?"
asked Buxton.

Bear scratched his head.
He'd quite like a gigantic chocolate cookie or a pet alien.
But he wasn't sure his mummy would let him
have either of those.

So, for three **long** days,
Flora, Buxton and Bear patiently waited,
and waited, and waited for Bear's
tooth to fall out.

But nothing happened.

Each day, Bear wiggled
and wobbled his tooth,
but it just wouldn't budge.

"Do you want me to pull it out?"
asked Buxton.
"My Dad's got a special toolbox
with all sorts of wonderful
things that might help."

"No!" shouted Flora.
"My mummy says you must
absolutely **never**,
ever pull a tooth out."

Bear looked miserable as he bit on an apple.

"This tooth is never, **ever**
going to come out...

And I'm never, **ever** going to get a coin...

And then I'll never, **ever** buy something special."

"Bear! **IT'S GONE!**"
shouted Flora.

Bear looked in the mirror – his tooth had finally come out!

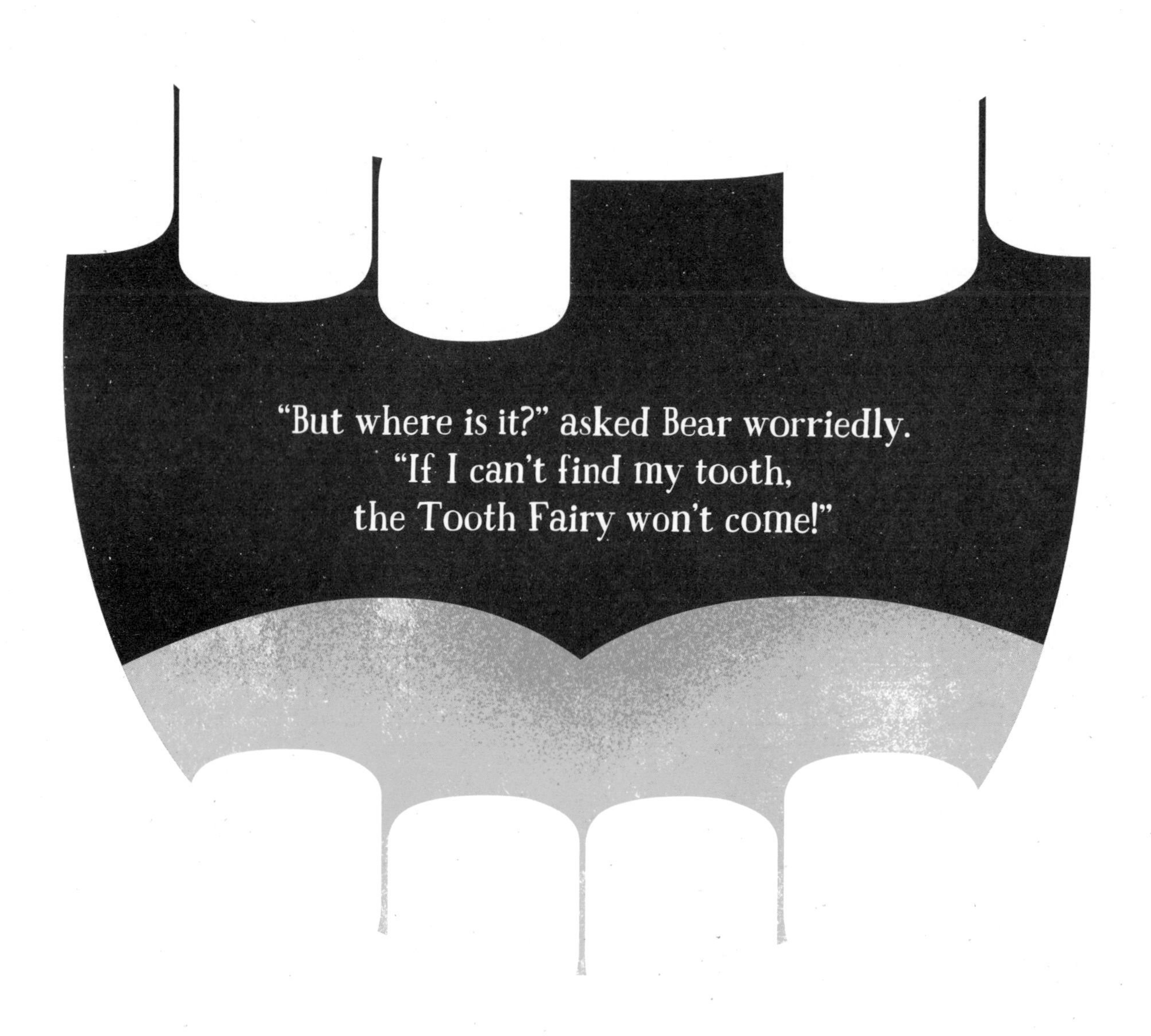

"But where is it?" asked Bear worriedly. "If I can't find my tooth, the Tooth Fairy won't come!"

The trio searched high and low
for the missing tooth – until Flora found it,
stuck in Bear's apple!

That night, Bear got ready for bed early.
He brushed his teeth as usual, and then placed the tooth
under his pillow. He squeezed his eyes tightly shut
so he could fall asleep really quickly.

The next morning,
much to Bear's delight,
there was a bright, shiny coin
under his pillow!

Bear knew right away
what he was going to spend it on,
and so he headed off to the shops with
his shiny coin in his pocket.

When Bear returned home, Flora and Buxton were excited to see what he'd bought.

"So... did you buy a **gigantic chocolate cookie?"** asked Flora.

"Did you buy a **pet alien?"** squealed Buxton, as he jumped up and down with delight.

"No," said Bear.

"I bought a... **telescope!**" said Bear excitedly.

"So I'll always be able to see
my most favourite tooth!"

Other titles in the

Flora, Buxton & Bear

Leap Book Library

www.fourthwallpublishing.com

First published in Great Britain in 2018 by Fourth Wall Publishing

ISBN: 978-1-910851-63-0

www.fourthwallpublishing.com
2 Riverview Business Park, Shore Wood Road, Bromborough, Wirral, Merseyside CH62 3RQ
A catalogue record for this book is available from the British Library
Printed in China